But Hopp was harder to convince . . .
"I just don't want to be a prince!"

I am NOT a Prince

Written by
Rachael Davis

Illustrated by
Beatrix Hatcher

ORCHARD

Beneath a fog of silver mist
Live magic frogs who'll soon be kissed.
Each springtime underneath the moon,
These frogs transform in the lagoon.

WANT
TO BE A
PRINCE?

HOP
THIS
WAY!

The others stared at Hopp agog.
"But it's the DUTY of a frog!"
"Oh no," said Hopp, **"It's not for me.**
That's not what I am meant to be."

The other frogs croaked in dismay –
"Then you must leave this place today!"

So Hopp set off towards the stream,
A lonely frog with one big dream.

LONELY PEAK

NO-RETURN COVE

SORROW SPRINGS

GHOSTLY WOOD

The lily pad rocked to and fro.
Oh, which way was it best to go?

A raging storm lit up the sky.
Hopp saw a mouse go running by.
"Please help!" cried Mouse. **"Owl's chasing me!"**
And scurried up a nearby tree.

Hopp leapt up high, to Owl's surprise.
**"Go pick on someone your own size!
Poor Mouse is tiny next to you!"**
And with a screech, away Owl flew.

"Oh, thank you, Frog. That owl was mean.
You are the kindest prince I've seen!"
The little frog flushed rosy red.
"Oh, I am **NOT** a prince," Hopp said.

As Hopp kept sailing down the stream,
A grizzly bear let out a scream.
"Help! HELP!" cried Bear. "My bum is stuck!
I tripped and fell. Oh, what BAD LUCK . . ."

Hopp gripped the beehive nice and tight
And tugged and pulled with froggy might.
"It's almost off," gasped tired Hopp,
And finally there came a . . .

"Oh, thank you, Frog. I'm in your debt.
You are the strongest prince I've met!"
But with a firm shake of the head,
"Oh, I am **NOT** a prince," Hopp said.

Before too long, Hopp saw dark smoke.
Was that the smell of burning oak?
A dragon squealed and flipped and flapped.
"Oh, help! Please, help! My baby's trapped!"

Poor Dragon clearly had the flu.
"Look out! There's more! Ah . . . ah . . .

. . . AH-CHOO!"

Hopp fearlessly
swung from a vine
And rescued Baby
just in time!

"Oh, thank you, Frog.
Though you are small,
You are the bravest prince of all!"
The little frog felt teary eyed.
"Oh, I am **NOT** a prince," Hopp sighed.

As darkness fell, the forest slept . . .
Except for Hopp, who sat and wept.
"I'm not a prince – they've got it wrong!
Oh where, oh where, do I belong?"

But little did Hopp know that fate
Had led straight to . . .

. . . a rainbow gate!

A sign read:

WELCOME!
COME INSIDE.
HERE DREAMS
COME TRUE.
FEAR NOT!
DON'T HIDE!

The front gate had been left ajar.
Hopp tiptoed in and then . . .

TA - DA!

A dazzling wizard, fair and kind,
Appeared and asked, **"What's on your mind?"**

"Nobody understands," Hopp cried,
"I want to be myself with pride.
Does all the world think I should be
A magic prince, except for me?"

The wizard touched a crystal ball.
Hopp's journey danced across the hall.
The wizard smiled, **"In many ways,
You've acted like a prince for days:**

You saved poor Mouse and set Bear free!

You rescued Dragon from a tree!"

"Please STOP!"
cried Hopp. "I've had enough!
I did love doing all that stuff,
But . . .

"...I am NOT a PRINCE!"

Hopp said.

"Well, tell me
what you *are* instead."

"**At last!**" Hopp cried, and gave a cheer,
Then whispered in the wizard's ear.
The wizard listened and could see
Who Hopp was truly meant to be.
"**You've shown great strength and courage too.
And now, here is my gift to you . . .**"

At the lagoon, the frogs felt blue.

Oh, where was Hopp? They wished they knew.

They'd judged their caring friend too fast,

And hoped Hopp would come home at last.

Then through the mist they saw a light.
A golden beam was shining bright.

Out of the bushes came a . . .

"BO

"What kind of princely prince are you?"

"Oh, I am **NOT** a prince," Hopp cried.
"I am **myself**," Hopp croaked with pride.
"Just look at me, and take a guess.
I've become . . .

PRINCESS!"

The mist was gone from Frog Lagoon!
They bopped and hopped beneath the moon.
And best of all, now frogs each spring . . .

. . . may transform into
ANYTHING!

For Elodie & Felicity - R.D.

For Alice, Mum, Dad, Mabel & Bumble - B.H.

ORCHARD BOOKS
First published in Great Britain in 2022
by The Watts Publishing Group
1 3 5 7 9 10 8 6 4 2

Text © Rachael Davis, 2022
Illustrations © Beatrix Hatcher, 2022

A CIP catalogue record for this book is available from the British Library.

HB ISBN 978 1 40836 225 9
PB ISBN 978 1 40836 226 6

Printed and bound in China

MIX
Paper from
responsible sources
FSC® C104740

Orchard Books
An imprint of Hachette Children's Group
Part of The Watts Publishing Group Limited
Carmelite House, 50 Victoria Embankment,
London EC4Y 0DZ

An Hachette UK Company
www.hachette.co.uk
www.hachettechildrens.co.uk